W9-BNR-460

For Emma Dryden, my magic touch

Kane Miller, A Division of EDC Publishing

Text and illustrations copyright © Michelle Nelson-Schmidt 2011

All rights reserved.

For information contact:
Kane Miller, A Division of EDC Publishing
PO Box 470663
Tulsa, OK 74147-0663
www.kanemiller.com
www.edcpub.com
www.usbornebooksandmore.com

Library of Congress Control Number: 2010941502

Manufactured by Regent Publishing Services, Hong Kong
Printed May 2018 in ShenZhen, Guangdong, China

Paperback ISBN: 978-1-61067-042-5
Hardcover ISBN: 978-1-61067-157-6

Cats, Cats!

Michelle Nelson-Schmidt

Cats, cats, are everywhere.
Look at all the cats out there!

fluffy

Fluffy cat, fluffy cat, you're silky to touch.
Everyone loves to pet you so much!

cat

nosy

Nosy cat, nosy cat, curious as can be.
Looking at everything, there’s so much to see!

timid

Timid cat, timid cat, under the bed.
Won't you come out, even to be fed?

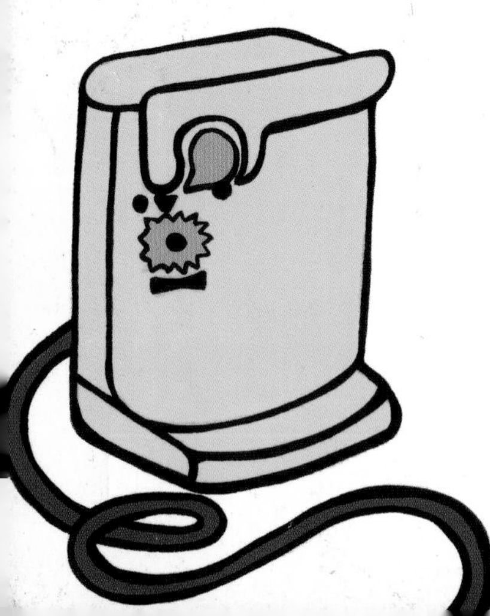

cat

Big cat, big cat, you’re so large.
All the dogs know who’s really in charge!

cat

purring

Purring cat, purring cat, what makes you grin?
Is it the warm, cozy bed you're sleeping in?

cat

Sneaky

Sneaky cat, sneaky cat, in the clean clothes.
Can't you find a new place to doze?

Brave cat, brave cat, climbing so high.
Are you chasing birds up in the sky?

pudgy

Pudgy cat, pudgy cat, you've snuck a big treat.
Now look at the mess all over your feet!

sleepy

Sleepy cat, sleepy cat, napping all day.
Would some of these toys get you to play?

cat

Angry cat, angry cat, why are you so mad?
You're swishing your tail; what is so bad?

cat

hungry

Hungry cat, hungry cat, with such a loud meow.
You're waking me up to feed you right now!

cat

silly

Silly cat, silly cat, tangled with glee.
Do you need help to get yourself free?

cat

cats, cats!

Little girl, little boy,
reading this book.

Which cat are you like?
Take a look!